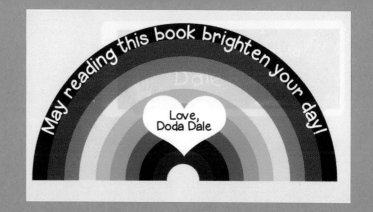

May reading this book brighten your day!

Love,
Doda Dale

Tefilat HaDerech
The Traveler's Prayer

תְּפִילַת הַדֶּרֶךְ

Adapted by Joshua Buchin

Illustrated by Woody Miller

For Poppop,
who told me stories
and took me on adventures.

———————

Tefilat HaDerech: The Traveler's Prayer

Copyright © 2012 by Joshua Buchin

Illustrated by Woody Miller

Design and Layout by Inna Inker Goldshteyn

Printed in The United States

EKS Publishing Co.
PO Box 9750
Berkeley, CA 94709-0750
email: orders@ekspublishing.com
Phone: (510) 251-9100
Fax: (510) 251-9102

www.ekspublishing.com

ISBN 978-0-939144-68-6 (paperback)
ISBN 978-0-939144-69-3 (hardcover)
First Printing, May 2012

Library of Congress Control Number: 2012937559

2000 BCE

c. 1900 BCE: Lech Lecha

1000 BCE

100 BC

Please God, our God,
and God of all that is,

100 CE   1000 CE   2000 CE

2000 BCE

1000 BCE

100 BC

c. 1280 BCE: Exodus from Egypt

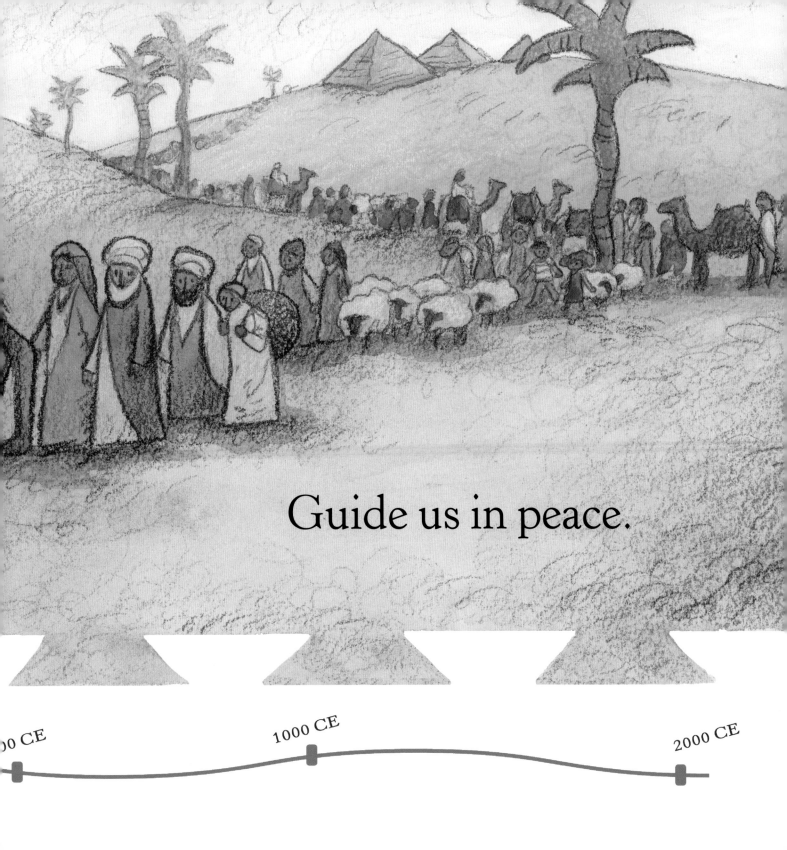

Guide us in peace.

2000 BCE

1000 BCE

100 BC

c. 1240 BCE: Conquest of Canaan

Lead us to our desired destination, always returning us to our homes.

2000 BCE

1000 BCE

100 BC

587 BCE: Babylonian Exile

Rescue us from all the trouble in our lives and in the world.

00 CE   1000 CE   2000 CE

Bless the work
of our hands.

2000 BCE   1000 BCE   100 BC'

c. 100: Jewish Traders in India and China

2000 BCE   1000 BCE   100 BCE

Allow us to find compassion and to live in tranquility.

1000 CE

2000 CE

1066: Jews Settle in England

2000 BCE

1000 BCE

100 BCE

Listen to our cries when we need You.

1492: Expulsion from Spain

2000 BCE   1000 BCE   100 BCE

You are a
God who hears those
who call out to You.

c. 1500 – c. 1940: Eastern
European Shtetls

00 CE   1000 CE   2000 CE

2000 BCE   1000 BCE   100 BCE

Blessed are You, God,
who listens to prayers.

0 CE   1000 CE   2000 CE

c. 1900: Jews
Arrive in America

May God bless and protect you.

2000 BCE   1000 BCE   100 BC

00 CE   1000 CE   2000 CE

**1948: Founding of
the State of Israel**

2000 BCE   1000 BCE   100 BCE

May God's love shine
on you at all times.

00 CE

1000 CE

2000 CE

c. 1980 - c. 1990: Rescue
of Soviet and Ethiopian Jews

May God always
guard your journeys
and return you
home safely.

c. 1900 BCE: Lech Lecha

Genesis tells the story of the first Jewish journey: Abraham and Sarah's departure from their home. Thus began the fulfillment of God's promise that the Jewish people would become a great and holy nation.

c. 1280 BCE: Exodus from Egypt

The Jewish journey from slavery to freedom has served as a model and inspiration for oppressed people throughout the world.

c. 1240 BCE: Conquest of Canaan

The Jewish people, under the leadership of Joshua, reclaimed the land of their ancestors, Canaan.

587 BCE: Babylonian Exile

After the destruction of the First Temple in Jerusalem, Babylonia became an intellectual and spiritual center for the Jewish people. The legacy of this era is the Babylonian Talmud.

c. 100: Jewish Traders

Although Jews had lived in diverse places for hundreds of years, the start of the new Millennium saw a large influx of Jewish travelers who strengthened existing communities in places such as China and India.

1066: Jews Settle in England

During the Middle Ages, Jews lived briefly in England. Although originally welcomed, the Jews were expelled in 1290.

1492: Expulsion from Spain

One of the darkest periods of Jewish history saw the forced conversion and expulsion of what had been a large and prosperous Jewish community.

c. 1500 - c. 1940: Eastern European Shtetls

For hundreds of years Jews living in Eastern Europe thrived. The rich environment produced religious, artistic and cultural innovations that continue to affect the modern Jewish landscape.

c. 1900: Jews Arrive in America

In search of a better world, many Jews moved to America in the 20th century. While their lives were initially difficult, they soon became a vibrant, rich, and diverse Jewish community.

c. 1980 - c. 1990: Rescue of Soviet and Ethiopian Jews

After years of hardship, members of these Jewish communities immigrated to countries with social, religious, and economic freedom.

1948: Founding of the State of Israel

Making the dream of a "land of milk and honey" a reality, the establishment of the State guaranteed a Jewish homeland for future generations.

Today, Jews continue to travel and live all over the world.

תְּפִילַת הַדֶּרֶךְ

Tefilat HaDerech:
The Traveler's Prayer

יְהִי רָצוֹן מִלְּפָנֶיךָ, יי אֱלֹהֵינוּ וֵאלֹהֵי אֲבוֹתֵינוּ, שֶׁתּוֹלִיכֵנוּ לְשָׁלוֹם, וְתַצְעִידֵנוּ לְשָׁלוֹם,

May it be Your will, God, our God and the God of our ancestors, to escort us to peace, and lead us to peace.

וְתַדְרִיכֵנוּ לְשָׁלוֹם,
וְתַגִּיעֵנוּ לִמְחוֹז חֶפְצֵנוּ לְחַיִּים וּלְשִׂמְחָה וּלְשָׁלוֹם, וְתַחֲזִירֵנוּ לְבֵיתֵנוּ לְשָׁלוֹם,

Guide us to peace, and guide us to our desired destination in life, and to joy, and to peace, and return us to our homes in peace.

וְתַצִּילֵנוּ מִכַּף כָּל אוֹיֵב וְאוֹרֵב וְאָסוֹן בַּדֶּרֶךְ, וּמִכָּל מִינֵי פֻּרְעָנִיּוֹת הַמִּתְרַגְּשׁוֹת לָבוֹא לָעוֹלָם,

Rescue us from the hand of every enemy, ambush, and catastrophe on the way, and from all kinds of trouble that happens to come to the world.

וְתִשְׁלַח בְּרָכָה בְּמַעֲשֵׂה יָדֵינוּ, וְתִתְּנֵנוּ לְחֵן וּלְחֶסֶד וּלְרַחֲמִים בְּעֵינֶיךָ וּבְעֵינֵי כָל רוֹאֵינוּ,

Send blessings to the work of our hands, and grant us grace, loving-kindness, and compassion in Your eyes, and in the eyes of all who see us.

וְתִשְׁמַע קוֹל תַּחֲנוּנֵינוּ, כִּי אֵל שׁוֹמֵעַ תְּפִלָּה וְתַחֲנוּן אַתָּה. בָּרוּךְ אַתָּה יי, שׁוֹמֵעַ תְּפִלָּה.

Hear our requests, because You are a God who hears prayer and requests. Blessed are You God, who hears prayer.

יְבָרֶכְךָ יי וְיִשְׁמְרֶךָ. יָאֵר יי פָּנָיו אֵלֶיךָ וִיחֻנֶּךָּ. יִשָּׂא יי פָּנָיו אֵלֶיךָ וְיָשֵׂם לְךָ שָׁלוֹם.

May God bless you and keep you safe. May God shine God's presence on you and be gracious to you. May God turn God's face towards you and give you peace.

פרק קכא

שִׁיר לַמַּעֲלוֹת
אֶשָּׂא עֵינַי אֶל־הֶהָרִים מֵאַיִן יָבֹא עֶזְרִי: עֶזְרִי מֵעִם יי עֹשֵׂה שָׁמַיִם וָאָרֶץ: אַל־יִתֵּן לַמּוֹט רַגְלֶךָ אַל־יָנוּם שֹׁמְרֶךָ: הִנֵּה לֹא יָנוּם וְלֹא יִישָׁן שׁוֹמֵר יִשְׂרָאֵל: יי שֹׁמְרֶךָ יי צִלְּךָ עַל־יַד יְמִינֶךָ: יוֹמָם הַשֶּׁמֶשׁ לֹא־יַכֶּכָּה וְיָרֵחַ בַּלָּיְלָה: יי יִשְׁמָרְךָ מִכָּל־רָע יִשְׁמֹר אֶת־נַפְשֶׁךָ: יי יִשְׁמָר־צֵאתְךָ וּבוֹאֶךָ מֵעַתָּה וְעַד־עוֹלָם:

Psalm 121

A Song for Going Up
I will raise my eyes to the mountains. From where will my help come? My help comes from God, the Maker of heaven and earth. God will not allow your foot to wobble. Your guardian will never doze. Behold! The Guardian of Israel will never doze and will never sleep. God is your guard. God is your shade, by your right hand. By day the sun will not beat down upon you, nor the moon at night. God will guard you from all evil. God will guard your life. God will guard your going and your coming, from now until forever.

About *Tefilat HaDerech*
The Traveler's Prayer

Tefilat HaDerech, The Traveler's Prayer, offers comfort to us as we embark on the journeys that take us through life. Historically, traveling was a dangerous process, one that required a long leave of absence from society and family as one moved from the known to the unknown, all the while traveling through uncertain territory. Our ancient Rabbis were aware of the potential danger firsthand. Often, they would travel long distances to teach, study, or work.

Conscious of the potential pitfalls associated with travel, the Rabbis taught that "one who travels in a place with wild animals and robbers should pray a short prayer." The Rabbis then expanded this, saying that "all who go out on the road must pray The Traveler's Prayer." In the Talmud, the Rabbis provide the text as we generally see it today in *siddurim* (prayerbooks). Although the bulk of the prayer was fixed almost two thousand years ago, different communities have the custom of embellishing this basic prayer with additional Biblical passages.

Considering how many journeys the Jewish people have taken throughout history, by choice as well as by force, it seems only fitting that we have a prayer to mark those adventures.

Although travel today is less perilous and more commonplace than ever, this prayer is still relevant. Remembering the role that God and the Jewish tradition play in our lives can help ease the transitions and hurdles that traveling can present. If we remember that we are not alone—that we are surrounded by community, part of a continuum of Jewish history, and sheltered by God—all of our journeys will be sanctified in holiness.

Nesia Tova, Happy Travels!

Joshua Buchin